Her Own Road

this book belongs to

____

____

There once was a little girl who tiptoed over cobblestones, dreamt of breezing through the clouds on hot air balloon rides, caught every dream, and held the earth's tears like a waterfall. She had no real home.

One afternoon in June, she tripped on the sidewalk and fell down. She got a tiny cut on her leg, a bit larger than a paper cut. She felt scared.

Night began to fall. She was alone with no one to pick her up and the sky grew purple and dark.

When the stars came out, she followed some fireflies who led her on her path. She was no longer tiptoeing, but began to walk.

She looked up at the red blinking lights that pilots use to conduct a safe flight, which comforted her as she walked.

Enamored with the sky once again, she wanted to sleep just to live in her dreamworld, but she knew that she had to get somewhere quickly to feel safe in order to have a home.

The fireflies were silent, but sweet. They led her to a blue roan quarter horse in the forest. Once there, she found a marigold flower which healed her cut when she touched it.

It was dark, but the horse's eyes were as bright as the fireflies.' The fireflies said goodbye, flying on to help someone else. When she looked in the quarter horse's eyes, she felt alive. She only had $.50 in her pocket and offered him $.25 for a quick ride. He whispered that no payment was needed.

She rode on his back and felt the wind like a waterfall rushing through her black hair. She galloped with no fear, and laughed about her former little cut.

After traveling with the blue roan, she knew that she found her home with him. It was getting late and she still hadn't eaten all day, so the roan asked a fairy friend to bring her a burger, fries, and a cupcake.

The fairy used her magic wand to give the roan a pair of wings!

'Thank you," she said to them both. "You're the home I never had," she whispered to the blue roan. They flew into the evening sky where a hot air balloon was awaiting them. She slept in the basket that night with the blue roan flying next to her.

The ...

..End

Nicole Ann Sobers was born in New Jersey and now lives in the Southeastern United States. "Her Own Roan" is her debut book. She loves working from home, music, movies, art, spending time in nature and with friends, and of course, horses.

Ruby Katana Gates

Ruby Katana Gates grew up in Western North Carolina with her three brothers and an imagination as playmates. To this day she dwells in her land of fairytales and knights, never ceasing with new creative ideas that may one day finally rest on paper.

how to draw a hot air ballon

Practice here!

Color me

www.ingramcontent.com/pod-product-compliance
Lightning Source LLC
LaVergne TN
LVHW071114160826
845679LV00004B/1068

* 9 7 9 8 8 4 6 4 4 1 0 0 2 *